Once upon a . . . pirate

Nick Page

How to use this book

First read the cast list and choose your characters.

Next complete the story. Place a sticker wherever there is a symbol on the page.
Look carefully at the symbol and choose a sticker from the section of the
sticker sheets marked by the same symbol.

When you have placed all the stickers, read the story to a friend!

Remove the stickers and store them in the plastic pockets
at the front of the book.

Choose a different combination of characters, places, and things
each time you read the book!

make
believe
ideas

The Cast List

Uncle Hook lost his hand fighting Moby Duck, the great white mallard of the sea. He loves cats.

Uncle Sandovar is wild and brave. He once stayed in the swimming pool a whole hour after the lifeguards told him to get out.

Uncle Redbeard would have a bright red beard if he grew one. But beards make him break out in a rash, so he just pretends.

Patches gives away her treasure to poor people, but then has to ask them to lend her money for the bus.

Gentleman George used to be a traffic officer, but turned to piracy because it was less frightening.

Blue Bert is cheerful, friendly and brave. He has a fine singing voice and can say, "hello, shipmate," in 26 languages!

Mad Maggie ran away to sea to escape being forced to wear tights. Well, you would, too, wouldn't you?

One-eyed Sam lost his eye in a cake-making accident, but his good eye can see twice as far as anyone else's.

Scarface McGraw got his scar when he cut himself shaving. But he prefers people to think he got it fighting in a duel.

Black Dog adores the color black. The fact that he has curly blonde hair has driven him mad with rage.

Mad Bernard Podmore is mad, vicious and heavily armed. He eats only bacon-flavored chips and giggles during funerals.

The Masked Terror is a deadly shot and has a strange obsession with grapes. His real name is a mystery.

Mickey Macaw knows the words to over 15 sea shanties, many of which are very rude and can only be sung late at night.

Polly Parrot likes cheese and chatters away in Dutch. No one knows how old she is.

Hot Harry likes peanuts and songs played on the accordion. He was captured during a raid in Africa.

Billy was an ordinary boy. He liked playing with his ⚓ . But he and his family were very poor and they never had enough money to buy nice clothes to wear, or food to eat — especially ⚓ , which was his favorite. One day, Billy got a letter through the mail from his ✺

"Dear Billy," it said. "I need your help. Would you like to earn some  ?

I need a cook on my ship. It is the .

We're going on a voyage to find some

P.S. You'll need a

Billy was absolutely amazed! His  was also a PIRATE!

The next day, Billy rushed down to the docks, where all the ships were. He saw ✸ standing on the deck of a large sailing ship. He had a ⚔ on his shoulder. "Welcome aboard the ⚔, shipmate!" he said. "Where are we going?" asked Billy. "To find the lost ⛵ of Captain Blood!" said his uncle. He showed Billy a map with an island.

"You go to this ⛵, then to this ⛵," explained his uncle. "Then, according to this map, the treasure is under a ⛵ We've got to hurry, in case ⚔ gets there first! He's my enemy! You can always spot him because he has a "

"First, you'll need to get some supplies," said the captain. "Go and buy yourself some proper pirate equipment!" And he gave Billy some   . Billy went into a shop and bought , a and a  . He was ready to be a pirate!

Back on the ship, Billy met the crew.

There was ✷, who was the first mate. There was ✷, who steered the ship. There was ✷, who hauled up the sails. They gave Billy a and a so that he looked like a real pirate. That evening, as soon as the tide changed, they set sail. Soon, they were far out at sea.

9

Billy worked hard at being the cook. He had to get up very early in the morning and start work. For breakfast, Billy cooked them ⚓. For lunch he cooked them ⚓. And for dinner he cooked them ⚓. And in the evening, of course, they all drank ⚓

Then they would sit and sing songs about the sea while the ⚔ played the ⚓. The best singer was ✹. Billy spent the rest of the time teaching ⚔ tricks. Their favorite was when Billy would throw his ⚓ in the air. The bird would catch it in his beak, fly around the ship twice and then hand it back to Billy!

ne morning, when they were a long way out into the ocean, Billy woke up. He went out to start cooking some  for breakfast. But then he noticed something: everything was deadly quiet. "Something is not right!" he whispered to himself.

Quietly, he crept up onto the deck.
There, he saw a strange man, wearing
a ___ and ___. He had a ___
It was ⚔! He had captured the crew and
tied them all to the mast. He was pointing
a ___ at them. Only ⚔ had escaped
and was sitting on a barrel. "Where's the
treasure map?" ⚔ asked ✸.
"Tell me or I'll make you
walk the plank!"

Billy had to act quickly! Silently, he crept up behind ⚔ and then BANG! He kicked the high into the air. ⚔ thought it was a ⚓ ! He dived down, grabbed it in his beak, flew twice round the ship and then gave it to Billy. Billy pointed the at the bad pirate.

"Let my friends go!" he said. "Or else I'll use this to turn you into ⚓." The crew cheered. Billy had rescued them all! They tied ⚔ up and locked him in the ship's prison. They all had a glass of ⚓ to celebrate. Suddenly, in the middle of the celebrations, ✸ pointed into the distance and shouted, "Land ahoy!"

 t was the treasure island. As soon as they could, they rowed ashore.

Then they got out the map and Billy used his 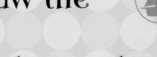 to find the 🚢 and the 🚢.

Then they saw the 🚢 and digging down, they discovered a treasure chest full of 🚢 and 🚢.

They had found the lost treasure of Captain Blood. They were rich! They set sail for home and soon they were back in Billy's hometown. "Thanks for helping us, Billy," said ✴ . "You've saved us all." And he gave Billy his share of the ⛵ .

"Thanks!" said Billy. "Now I can buy a new ⚓ and loads of ⚓ . It's my favorite!"

Choose your favorite stickers!

Uncle  Ship Food

Crew Weapon Drink

Villain Instrument Gear

Bird Treasure Money